Jack
and the
Beanstalk

PaRRagon

Bath · New York · Cologne · Melbourne · Delhi
Hong Kong · Shenzhen · Singapore

Four steps for enjoyable reading

Traditional stories and fairy tales are a great way to begin reading practice. The stories and characters are familiar and lively. Follow the steps below to help your child become a confident and independent reader:

Step 1
Read the story aloud to your child. Run your finger under the words as you read.

One day, Jack's mom said, "We have no money and nothing to eat. Take our cow to the market and sell it so that we can buy some food."
    Jack took the cow to the market. He swapped the cow for some magic beans.

4

Step 2
Look at the pictures and talk about what is happening.

Step 3

Read the simple text on the right-hand page together. When reading, some words come up again and again, such as **the**, **to**, **and**. Your child will quickly get to recognize these high-frequency words by sight.

Jack ran all the way home with his bag of beans.

Step 4

When your child is ready, encourage them to read the simple lines on their own.

One day, Jack's mom said, "We have no money and nothing to eat. Take our cow to the market and sell it so that we can buy some food."

Jack took the cow to the market. But instead of selling the cow, he swapped it for some magic beans.

Jack ran all the way home
with his bag of beans.

But when Jack's mom saw the
beans, she was cross.

"Silly boy!" shouted Jack's mom.
"Now we have no cow, no money,
and nothing to eat!"

She threw the beans into the
garden and sent Jack to bed.

Jack went off to bed. He was sad about the beans.

The next morning, Jack looked out of his window. There was a giant beanstalk in the garden! Jack was hungry. He climbed the beanstalk to look for some beans to eat.

He climbed up and up, into the clouds.

Jack went all the way
to the top of the giant
beanstalk.

At the top of the beanstalk, Jack found a giant castle. He knocked on the castle door. The cook opened the door.

"Please can I have something to eat?" said Jack.

The cook gave him some food. Then they heard footsteps.

"You must hide!" she cried. "The giant who lives here likes to eat little boys for his supper!"

Boom, boom, boom! Jack hid in
a cupboard.

The bad, greedy giant stomped into the kitchen.

"Fee-fi-fo-fum, I smell the blood of a little boy!" the giant shouted.

"Don't be silly," said the cook, "you smell sausages cooking."

Jack was scared. Would the giant
eat him?

The greedy giant ate his sausages.

"Bring me my gold!" roared the giant. The cook got his gold, and the greedy giant counted it.

Soon, the giant fell asleep. Jack popped out of the cupboard and grabbed a bag of gold!

Jack quickly climbed back down
the beanstalk with the bag of gold.

Jack's mom bought some food. But soon, all the gold was gone and they were hungry again. Jack climbed up the beanstalk again.

He hid in the castle. Soon, the greedy giant came into the kitchen.

"Fee-fi-fo-fum, I smell the blood of a little boy!" he shouted.

"Don't be silly," said the cook, "you smell your dinner."

The giant ate his food.

"Bring me my hen!" roared the greedy giant. The cook fetched a fat red hen. The hen laid a big golden egg!

As soon as the giant fell asleep, Jack popped out and grabbed the hen.

Jack climbed down the
beanstalk with the fat
red hen.

The next day, Jack climbed the beanstalk again. He hid in the castle and waited for the giant to come.

"Bring me my harp!" roared the giant. The cook got a golden harp. The harp sang to the giant. He fell asleep. Jack popped out and grabbed it. But the giant woke up.

"Fee-fi-fo-fum!" he cried.
"Stop! Come back, boy!"

Jack climbed down the beanstalk as fast as he could go. The giant chased after him.

Jack got to the bottom and grabbed an ax. He chopped down the beanstalk. Crash! The giant fell to the ground.

And that was the end of
the bad, greedy giant.